Content developed & packaged by Mojo Media, Inc.
Editor: Joe Funk
Creative Director: Jason Hinman

This book is available in quantity at special discounts for your group or organization.
For further information, contact:

Triumph Books
542 South Dearborn Street
Suite 750
Chicago, IL 60605
Phone: (312) 939-3330
Fax: (312) 663-3557

Printed in the United States of America
ISBN: 978-1-60078-217-6

Contents

David Beckham

Hometown: London, England
Club: Los Angeles Galaxy

The biggest international superstar in sports today is undoubtedly David Beckham. Coming from humble roots as a fan in London to becoming the face of his sport has been a long journey for Becks, but it's a destiny he has embraced with open arms.

The stunning midfielder was known for his booming and curving free kicks from his teen years, and he quickly moved up to the Manchester United Reserves to go along with occasional first-team appearances. He would also earn notice with the England U-21 side, which helped David become one of the most recognized up-and-comers in the soccer world.

His control of the game quickly made him a fixture in the Manchester United lineup, and by age 21 he had secured his place as a star of the team. He also became a regular with the senior national team, culminating in his nomination to the squad that competed in the 1998 World Cup.

Since, Beckham has been at the top of the soccer world and has become an international superstar. He has twice more played in the World Cup for England and has remained a regular on the squad even after leaving old club Real Madrid for the LA Galaxy, making him the first MLS player to play for England. Although he is no longer the captain of the international team, Becks has no intentions of leaving international play.

Since signing with LA, Beckham has exposed himself to an all-new audience in the United States. Even though he has reached his 30s and struggled with injuries David has shown no signs of slowing down and remains the most popular soccer player in the world.

"I think every player would like to reach this target but very few manage it; so you have to give David Beckham credit. He has done really well to achieve this. He's a great professional."

– England manager Fabio Capello on Beckham making his 100th appearance for England

Fast Stat:

6

Years that Beckham was captain of the English national team

Ht: 6' 0" • **Wt:** 165 • **DOB:** 5/2/75

Position: Midfield

2007–2008 salary:
$50 million (actual figure not disclosed)

Career goals/international caps:
76 club goals/100 caps

Personal homepage:
http://www.davidbeckham.com/

Did you know?: David and his wife Victoria have three sons.

As a kid: David, his parents, and two sisters were huge Manchester United fans, often travelling from London to Manchester to see them play.

Favorite foods: David enjoys eating Italian and Chinese food, but also loves English staple fish and chips.

Hobbies: David enjoys other sports, especially boxing and rugby. He says he would have liked to play professional cricket had he not become a soccer player.

Favorite music: Pop music, dance/house music, his wife Victoria, and Pavarotti

Kaka

Hometown: Brasilia, Brazil
Club: AC Milan

A member of the latest generation of South American players to excel in Europe, electrifying midfielder Kaka has enjoyed success after success in his career.

Coming from a stable, middle-class family in Brazil, Kaka and his brother were gifted from a young age. After attending a local academy at age eight, Kaka signed his first pro contract at age 13. His rise was swift, and within seven years he had been named to the 2002 World Cup squad for Brazil.

His time on that team would be frustrating, however, as Kaka observed more than he played. Only appearing in 18 minutes of action in one game, he returned to his club ready to become a star thanks to his new-found drive to be one of the best.

A star for AC Milan, Kaka is one of only a handful of young Brazilians enjoying immediate success in Europe, a role that is becoming progressively more difficult to attain. Returning to the World Cup in 2006, Kaka started the tournament off with a bang, scoring his team's only goal in their opening game win over Croatia. Unfortunately, the tournament went downhill from there – Kaka did not score again and Brazil was knocked out in the quarterfinals.

A man of deep religious conviction, Kaka spends much of his offseason donating time to help the poor. Since 2006 he has been an ambassador for the United Nations' World Food Program, providing hope for people worldwide.

Fast Stat:

62

Number of career goals in Kaka's first seven professional seasons

Ht: 6' 1" • **Wt:** 180 • **DOB:** 4/22/82

Position: Midfield

2007–2008 salary: $8.4 million

Career goals/international caps:
77 club goals/37 caps

Did you know?: Kaka was nearly paralyzed in a swimming accident when he was 18, but managed to make a full recovery.

As a kid: Kaka enjoyed playing soccer as a kid in the streets and on the beach, always teamed up with his brother.

Fun tidbit: Kaka's brother, Rodrigo, plays with him at AC Milan.

Hobbies: Kaka enjoys spending time with his wife and family, and playing beach soccer.

Favorite music: Gospel

"Kaka has been playing at this level for Brazil for four years now, he helps out in midfield and he is also a great example off the pitch. He's the complete player."
– Pele

Iker Casillas

Hometown: Madrid, Spain

Club: Real Madrid

For Iker Casillas, stopping the ball is all there is to soccer. As he sees it, his only job is to keep the ball from going into the net, no matter what it takes. Thanks to this dedication to his position, Casillas has arguably become the best goalkeeper in the world.

A native of Madrid, Iker has never spent a day playing club soccer away from Real Madrid. Whether it be at the youth level, the reserve level, or the senior team itself, Casillas has only played for Real Madrid; he hasn't even been loaned out to another club.

After a slow but steady rise to the first team, Casillas debuted for Real Madrid during the 1998-1999 season. The next year he became a starter in net, leading Real to a Champions League victory over national rival Valencia. Just four days past his nineteenth birthday, he was the youngest keeper of a Champions League champion ever.

Two seasons later, bad form saw Casillas lose his starting job, only to be called on in a Champions League final once more. Real Madrid proved triumphant again, beating Bayer Leverkuser 2-1. Casillas has been the starter ever since.

Casillas may be more notable for his international play with Spain. After becoming the starter due to injury at the 2002 World Cup, Casillas has been the national team's first choice keeper. He played again at the 2006 World Cup, captaining Spain twice. This year, he became the first player to be a keeper and captain his team to a European championship when Spain took Euro 2008.

"I like to remember my roots. It's about helping those kids from my town so they know that hard work pays off and they can do anything they set their minds to."

— Casillas on remembering where he came from

Fast Stat:

2017

The year that Iker is signed until by Real Madrid

Ht: 6' 1" • **Wt:** 170 • **DOB:** 5/20/81

Position: Goalkeeper

2008–2009 Salary: $9.5 million

Career Goals/International caps: 313 club appearances/75 international caps

Did you know?: With Spain's win at Euro 2008, Iker became the first keeper to captain his team to the European championship.

As a kid: Iker spent his entire childhood in the Real Madrid system, spending eight years there before making his senior team debut.

Fun tidbit: One of Iker's saves from the 2002 World Cup was named one of the 10 best saves of all time.

Hobbies: Iker enjoys hanging out with his teammates and driving his car.

Favorite music: Iker enjoys pop and hip hop.

Cesc Fabregas

Hometown: Barcelona, Spain
Club: Arsenal

One of the dynamic young players that will keep Spain at the top of European soccer for years to come, Cesc Fabregas has slowly carved a starring career for himself at one of the Premier League's biggest clubs, Arsenal.

Born an FC Barcelona fan in his home country of Spain, Fabregas spent some time playing with Barca's youth academy as a kid. He regularly scored more than 30 goals in a season, but when the time came to sign a professional contract, Arsenal swooped in and signed Fabregas before any Spanish club could.

The pairing has not always been smooth. It has taken Fabregas several years to develop into a top-flight player, but such are the growing pains for a young talent. He was part of the Arsenal team that went undefeated in 2003–2004, but he did not receive a winner's medal since he did not play in any leaue games that year for the Gunners. Fabregas finally began appearing in first team games the next year, and by 2005–2006 was a steady presence in the Arsenal midfield.

Fabregas' style has become more aggressive in recent seasons, attributed to becoming more comfortable with the English style of play. He finally broke out in 2007–2008, scoring 13 times over 45 appearances in all competitions that Arsenal played in, including six goals in the Champions League.

He has also become a fixture in Spain's international squad. Although he does not always start, Fabregas is an important part of the team. He played in the World Cup in 2006 at the age of just 19, starting twice and recording an assist in the tournament. Fabregas scored his first international goal at Euro 2008, added a shootout winner in the quarterfinals against Italy, and was named to the Team of the Tournament for his play.

Fast Stat:

16

Cesc's age when he made his first career appearance for Arsenal, making him the youngest player to ever play for the team

Ht: 5' 10" • **Wt:** 150 • **DOB:** 4/4/87

Position: Central Midfield

2008–2009 salary: $4.5 million

Career goals/international Caps:
14 club goals/24 international caps

Personal homepage:
www.cescfabregassoler.com

Did you know?: Arsenal is the only club that Cesc has played for professionally.

As a kid: Cesc was a huge FC Barcelona fan as a kid; he went to his first game with his grandfather when he was just nine months old.

Fun tidbit: Cesc is a big supporter of the Teenage Cancer Trust, a charity for helping teens with cancer live better lives.

Hobbies: Cesc enjoys hosting TV programs during the offseason.

Favorite music: R&B and hip hop.

Ronaldinho

Hometown: Porto Alegre, Brazil
Club: AC Milan

A two-time World Player of the Year, Ronaldinho is arguably the most popular soccer player in the world, given his immense European and South American followings. Generating more marketing revenue than even David Beckham, Ronaldinho is so popular he even has a comic book based on him. Rising from the millions of Brazilian children playing beach soccer and futsal in his home country, Ronaldinho's talents were evident from a young age. During a youth league game, he completed an impressive feat by scoring every one of his team's goals in a 23–0 win. Already a small media sensation for his abilities by age eight, he would not be missed by national team coaches. Ronaldinho first competed at the under-15 level for his homeland in 1995, several years after turning professional with a local squad. Already employing some of the stepovers, pace, and ball control that would become hallmarks of his professional career, Ronaldinho rose quickly through the ranks.

It would take a move to Europe to solidify Ronaldinho's place as an elite athlete. He played in France starting in 2001 but it was not until after the 2002 World Cup that he attracted more attention. Recently, Ronaldinho made the move away from Barcelona to AC Milan, where he wears number 80. He has earned two FC FIFA Player of the Year awards with Barcelona, leading them to domestic and Champion's League crowns to go along with his personal success. Recently, Ronaldinho became a citizen of Spain and he now holds dual citizenship for Spain as well as his homeland of Brazil.

Fast Stat:

23

Goals scored by Ronaldinho in a 23–0 youth team win

Ht: 5' 11" • **Wt:** 175 • **DOB:** 3/21/80

Position: Attacking Midfielder

2007–2008 Salary: $11.4 million

Career Goals/International Caps:
124 goals/62 caps

Personal Homepage:
http://www.ronaldinhogaucho.com/

Did you know?: The nickname Ronaldinho literally means "little Ronaldo."

As a kid: Ronaldinho was seemingly born with a ball between his feet. He loved spending time at the beach, playing beach games including volleyball and soccer.

Favorite foods: Ronaldinho loves steak and beans — but has a special place in his heart for when it is made by his mother.

Hobbies: Ronaldinho loves playing video games (he's a FIFA Soccer coverboy) and spending time with his family.

Favorite music: Samba music

"Every day I wake up with a new dream which I try to make come true."

– Ronaldinho on his daily motivations

Cristiano Ronaldo

Hometown: Madeira, Portugal
Club: Manchester United

Discovered by Manchester United manager Sir Alex Ferguson after a preseason exhibition match, Cristiano Ronaldo was one of Portugal's best-kept secrets throughout his youth years. Like most top-level professional players, Ronaldo became a solid player during his youth years, signing his first professional developmental deal at age 10. Quickly moving through the domestic league, Ronaldo soon found himself in the academy of the country's highest profile team, Sporting Lisbon.

After his performance in an under-17 youth tournament, professional teams throughout Europe began to take notice, although some, such as Liverpool, still thought he was not ready to advance. Although a very raw player coming up, by age 17 the Manchester United players and Ferguson had decided they'd rather play with him than against him.

Known for his intensity and occasional the-atrics and controversy on the field, no critic can doubt Cristiano's effort. Scoring multiple goals in several games during the 2006–2007 season, Cristiano was twice honored as the Premiership's Player of the Month during the season, a feat only three other players have accomplished.

Still scraping the top layers of his talent, at age 23 Cristiano Ronaldo is certain to be a fixture in the lineup for both Manchester United and Portugal for years to come. If his performance in the 2006 World Cup is any indication, Cristiano may be on the fast track to becoming one of the best players in the world.

"He's one of the most exciting young players I've ever seen."

— Manchester United manager Sir Alex Ferguson

Cristiano's age when Manchester United players convinced Manager Sir Alex Ferguson on a plane ride that they should sign him

Ht: 6' 1" • **Wt:** 180 • **DOB:** 2/5/85

Position: Midfield/Striker

2007–2008 Salary: $10.2 million

Career Goals/International caps:
69 club goals/55 caps

Did you know?: Cristiano scored two goals in his first senior game for Sporting Lisbon when he was just 16.

As a kid: A notable neighborhood street soccer player, Cristiano has been playing the game since age 3.

Favorite foods Cristiano Ronaldo enjoys any seafood, but mostly Portuguese codfish.

Hobbies: Watching movies, going on vacation, and the first day of soccer after a vacation.

Favorite music: Ronalda, dance music, electronica, and techno

Fernando Torres

Hometown: Madrid, Spain
Club: Liverpool

Already one of the top players in the world, Fernando Torres is a superstar on the rise. Having signed a youth deal with hometown club Atletico Madrid at the age of 11, Torres is accustomed to success. Stints with Spain's Under-17 and World Cup teams have simply added to an impressive list of accolades that Torres has earned at the age of 24. Discovered after a youth season in which he scored an impressive 55 goals from his striker position, Torres has been deadly in front of the net from his first kicks on.

Torres is known not only for his pace, but for his technical skill. A fast mover with or without the ball, Torres is right-footed but is equally adept at striking or ball handling with either foot. One of the deadliest threats near the goal in European soccer (either in the air or on the ground), Torres will lay low before striking with unfailing accuracy.

With five seasons with Atletico Madrid under his belt, it was a no-brainer that some of Europe's richest clubs would be after him. Eventually, Liverpool was the lucky squad, paying a club record transfer fee of over $50 million to Atletico for Torres' services. A man who never scores the same goal twice, Torres has quickly acclimated himself to the English game and is poised for even greater success.

"He is going to set the game alight in this division."

— Reading manager Steve Coppell after Torres netted a hat-trick in Carling Cup play

Fast Stat:

75

Goals Torres scored over five seasons in Spain, making him one of three men to accomplish the feat

Ht: 6' 1" • **Wt:** 170 • **DOB:** 3/20/84

Position: Striker

2007–2008 Salary: $9.56 million

Career Goals/International caps:
106 goals/47 caps

Personal Homepage:
www.fernando9torres.com

Did you know?: Liverpool paid a club record transfer fee to sign Torres.

As a kid: Torres enjoyed two main hobbies as young child — playing soccer and throwing things out his parents' window. He played goaltender until he was nine.

Favorite foods: Any pasta.

Hobbies: Away from the field, Fernando enjoys spending time with his girlfriend and reading (mostly books about soccer).

Favorite music: Rock

"Thierry Henry could take a ball in the middle of the park and score a goal that no one else in the world could score."

— Former Arsenal manager Arsene Wenger

Thierry Henry

Hometown: Paris, France

Club: FC Barcelona

One of the top strikers in the world for the last several years, Thierry Henry is not only a consistent goal-scorer — he enjoys new challenges as well. A World Cup Champion and an elite scorer, Henry is the definition of the team-oriented superstar.

After growing up up in a tough neighborhood in his native France, Henry signed his first professional contract for AS Monaco at the age of 13. He would stay with the club until 1998, when his three-goal performance in France's World Cup win saw transfer interest increase. After one season with Juventus, Henry would make his way to Arsenal, the club where he would have his greatest success.

The 2001–2002 season would be a special one for the club, as they won both the Premier League and the FA Cup while Henry garnered the first of his four Premier League scoring titles. After an undefeated run the next season, Arsenal would complete their most glorious era with another FA Cup in 2004.

Deadly from one-on-one attacking situations, Henry is known for his spectacular goals and ability to score from anywhere on the field. He is a first-rate free-kick taker and is the only man in Premier League history to score 20 or more goals in five straight seasons. With his work in England done, 2007 saw Henry back on the Continent, looking for more success with FC Barcelona.

Fast Stat:

174

Goals Henry scored during his eight years with Arsenal

Ht: 6' 2" • **Wt:** 183 • **DOB:** 8/17/77

Position: Striker

2007–2008 Salary: $12.4 million

Career Goals/International caps: 210 goals/100 caps

Did you know?: Henry led France in scoring when they won the World Cup in1998.

As a kid: Thierry grew up in a rough neighborhood in France but found solace in playing soccer.

Favorite foods: Chicken, rice, and Caribbean food.

Hobbies: Thierry is a political activist for many topics, most specifically his work against racism. He is also an avid NBA fan, and is close friends with San Antonio guard Tony Parker.

Favorite music: Zouk (slow Caribbean music), hip-hop, and rap

Steven Gerrard

Hometown: Whiston, England
Club: Liverpool

An inspiring and commanding player, Steven Gerrard may mean more to his team and its fans than any other player in the world. Born and raised near Liverpool, Gerrard has never played for any other squad and is the heart and soul of the current team. Having stated that he has no intentions of ever leaving the club, Gerrard provides a stability in the midfield that no other team can hope to replicate. Even more impressive, he remains among the top mid-fielders in the world and competes at an internationally high level as well.

Discovered as a school boy when just 8 years old, Gerrard has been a part of the fabric of Liverpool for nearly his entire life. Despite an injury-plagued junior career with the club, he would make his first-team debut at just 18 years old in 1998. By the next season, he had quickly established himself as a regular on a club destined for greatness in 2000–2001. Honored as the Young Player of the Year, Gerrard would score 10 goals for a team that would win the FA Cup, League Cup, and UEFA Cup.

Awards and accolades continued to follow for Gerrard, and in 2002 he was named to England's World Cup team. Unfortunately, surgery forced by injuries caused by a late growth spurt prevented Gerrard from competing. He would appear for England in the tournament in 2006, leading the team in scoring with his two goals.

"I'm a fan myself and I'm frustrated just as much as them when we get beat."

— Steven Gerrard on what Liverpool's success means to him

Fast Stat:

23

Goals Gerrard scored from his midfield position in 2005–2006

Ht: 6' 1" • **Wt:** 180 • **DOB:** 5/30/80

Position: Midfield

2007–2008 Salary: $12.75 million

Career Goals/International caps: 55 goals/48 caps

Personal Homepage: www.liverpoolfc.tv/team/squad/gerrard

Did you know?: Steven published an autobiography in 2006.

As a kid: Steven suffered from drastic growth spurts, stopping him from playing for long stretches at a time.

Favorite foods: Chicken, rice, and Caribbean food.

Hobbies: Steven enjoys collecting cars and driving them. He also enjoys golfing and playing pool.

Favorite music: Dance

Michael Ballack

Hometown: Goerlitz, Germany

Club: Chelsea

Ht: 6' 3" • **Wt:** 175 • **DOB:** 9/26/76

Position: Midfield

2007–2008 Salary: $12.8 million

Career Goals/International caps: 103 goals/79 caps

Personal Homepage: www.michael-ballack.com

Did you know?: Michael's learned vocation in secondary school was "Professional Football Player." He earned high marks.

As a kid: Michael earned some spending money by collecting waste paper and old bottles to trade in.

Fun tidbit: Ballack's favorite movie is *The Godfather*.

Hobbies: Away from the field, Ballack is a strong golfer and enjoys spending time with his family.

Favorite music: Pop, R&B, and soul

Germany's captain and premier midfielder, Michael Ballack has enjoyed nearly unequaled success in his soccer career. From his youth on, he always had a knack for scoring goals while not compromising his defensive responsibilities, a distinction he carries on today.

After first breaking into the professional ranks, Ballack immediately lit Germany's Bundesliga on fire. His goal scoring rate as a young professional has been nearly unequaled; not even David Beckham and Ronaldinho could match the young Ballack's totals in their early seasons. Named Player of the Year three times while playing at home, Ballack left Germany in 2006. Currently a top-flight midfielder with Chelsea in England, it has been nothing short of a successful run in club play for Ballack.

It is when wearing his country's colors, however, that Ballack truly shines. His huge goals against the United States and South Korea in the 2002 World Cup helped to key Germany to a runner-up appearance. Although he missed the final, Ballack had certainly turned heads within his national team. Named the captain for the 2006 tournament, Ballack quickly fell into his new role. Named Man of the Match twice during the World Cup, Michael helped the squad to a third-place finish.

"It's not enough to just possess talent, you also have to work hard to be able to reach your goals." – Ballack on the importance of talent

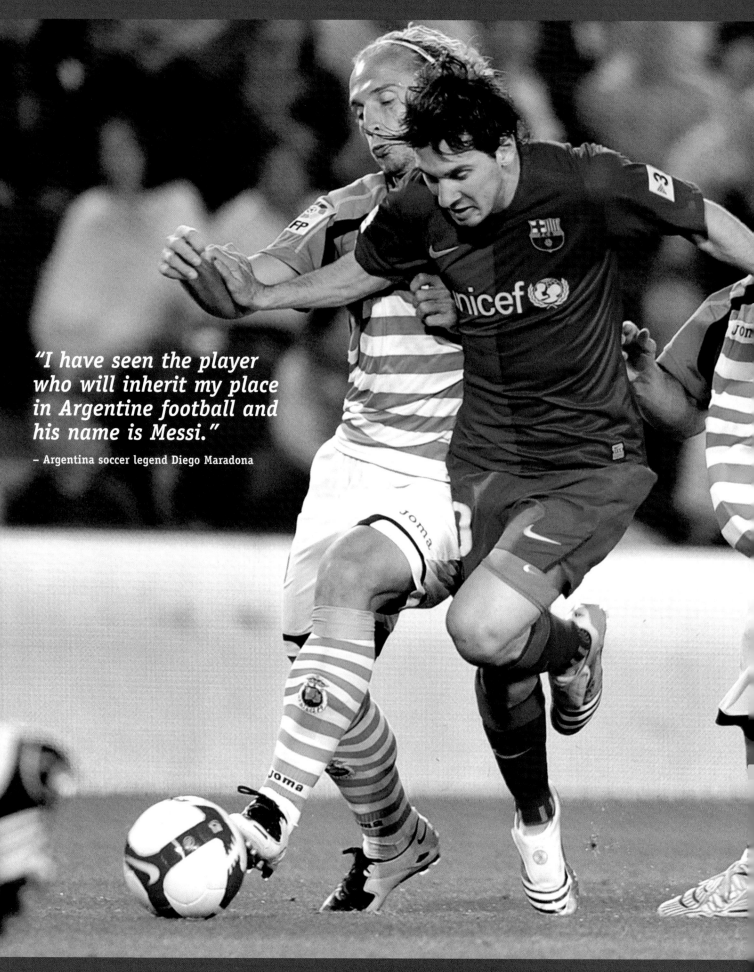

"I have seen the player who will inherit my place in Argentine football and his name is Messi."

– Argentina soccer legend Diego Maradona

Lionel Messi

Hometown: Rosario, Argentina
Club: FC Barcelona

A humble young man off of the soccer field, Lionel Messi is a dynamo on it. A spark plug that some say is worth more to his club than Ronaldinho, Messi is poised to be the face of soccer in the 21st century. Already drawing comparisons to legendary Argentine Diego Maradona, some by Maradona himself, Messi has some large shoes to fill at the tender age of 21.

Messi has been on the radar of the soccer world for several years already. Although he suffers from a growth hormone deficiency that prevents him from growing taller, Messi has always played a big game. Signing with FC Barcelona at the age of 13, Messi would make his debut with the side in 2003. At the age of 17, he would become the youngest player ever to score for the club in league play.

His great passing and seemingly perfect on-field relationship with teammates even spawned competition over Messi on the international level. Offered a chance to jump ship and compete with the Spanish international team, Messi declined, keeping his loyalties with his native Argentina.

A big-match player, Messi was named to Argentina's squad for the 2006 World Cup. Although he did not appear in the teams' first game and only came on as a late sub in the second, Messi was able to make a big impression. He would assist on a goal and score another, making him the youngest goalscorer of the tournament. In all, he would appear in four games in the World Cup, turning millions of heads around the world to see the skills of the small Argentine.

Fast Stat:

17

Messi's age when he scored his first goal for Barcelona

Ht: Ht: 5' 6" • **Wt:** 147 • **DOB:** 6/24/87

Position: Midfield/Striker

2007–2008 Salary: not available

Career Goals/International caps: 31 goals/18 caps

Did you know?: Lionel's middle name is Andres.

As a kid: Lionel moved to Spain when he was just 13 to pursue his dream of playing pro soccer.

Favorite foods: Argentine barbeque.

Hobbies: Lionel enjoys listening to traditional Argentine music and watching soccer on television.

Favorite music: Samba, cumbi, and dance

Wayne Rooney

Hometown: Liverpool, England
Club: Manchester United

Born and raised an Everton fan, young Wayne Rooney has been in the spotlight from a very young age. With a skill and passion for the game noticed by many, it seemed only fitting that Rooney's first professional club would be the one that he grew up following.

As a teen, Rooney found much success with the Everton youth squad that reached the Youth Cup final in 2002, earning him quick promotion to the first team. Against Arsenal later that year, Rooney would become the youngest goal scorer in the Premier League thanks to his first goal, one that prompted the television commentator to exclaim, "Remember the name Wayne Rooney!" Two seasons with Everton's first team and increasing pressure from local fans would cause the talented young Englishman to seek a transfer, and Manchester United was quick to snap him up.

Despite the increased media blitz surrounding him, Rooney has continued to excel at both the club and international levels. Rooney would become a mainstay for the English squad soon after his transfer to Manchester United, a feat no doubt helped by his impressive performances in the Euro 2004 tournament. Rooney would go on to make the World Cup squad in 2006, but had a disappointing tournament that would end with an unfortunate red card.

Wayne Rooney is one of the brightest young stars in the game today. He plays for the world's biggest soccer club and is already an internationally known star. Although he hasn't yet had major success on the world stage, fans are cautioned to remember the name Wayne Rooney.

Fast Stat:

3

Goals scored by Wayne in his first Manchester United match

Ht: : 5' 10" •**Wt:** 170 • **DOB:** 10/24/85

Position: Midfield/Striker

2007–2008 Salary: $5.5 million

Career Goals/International caps:
68 goals/33 caps

Personal Homepage:
www.waynerooney.com

Did you know?: When Wayne was called up for his first international game, he thought it was for the U-21 team.

As a kid: Wayne is the oldest of three children, and enjoyed spending time with his siblings.

Favorite foods: Spaghetti bolognese

Hobbies: Wayne enjoys playing video games, especially FIFA Soccer.

Favorite music: Eminem, 50 Cent

Frank Lampard

Hometown: London, England
Club: Chelsea

When you are playing with world-class individuals, when you are on top of your game it makes it look even better."

– Lampard on the importance of his teammates

One of the world's great under-rated players, Frank Lampard is a stalwart midfielder for Chelsea who in 2005 finished second behind only Ronaldinho for World Player of the Year honors. A player whose rise has been both slow and steady while at the same time spectacular, Lampard is a fixture for both Chelsea and the English national team.

After starting his career in promising fashion with basement dwellers West Ham United, Lampard was signed by Chelsea thanks to a hefty transfer fee in 2001. Bogged down in his first few years with Chelsea, Lampard would become a classic case of a late bloomer. He would seemingly add a new hat each year with Chelsea: playing every match in 2002, becoming a team leader and Player of the Month in 2003, and finally becoming the centerpiece of a championship squad in 2004–2005.

It was this magical season that earned Lampard his major world honors, scoring 13 goals in Chelsea's Premiership League winning season. Opponents would unanimously come together after games and praise Lampard, who was finally establishing himself as one of the world's top midfielders. With 71 goals, Lampard is currently the top scoring midfielder in club history and the top scoring player currently at the club.

Lampard has not been ignored by his country either, making appearances for the national team starting in 1999. He would not become a regular for several years, and missed out on important tournaments such as the 2002 World Cup.

Fast Stat:

13

Goals Frank has scored for England

Ht: 6' 0" • **Wt:** 165 • **DOB:** 6/20/78

Position: Midfield

2007–2008 Salary: $13.1 million

Career Goals/International caps:
95 goals/50 caps

Personal Homepage:
www.franklampard.com

Did you know?: Although signed by West Ham United, Lampard would actually score his first professional goal while on loan to Swansea City.

As a kid: Lampard grew up around the game, as both his father and uncle played and managed at the professional level.

Fun tidbit: Frank had his autobiography published in 2006.

Hobbies: Frank grew up with soccer and loved hanging around with his dad's team, West Ham.

Favorite music: Pop, dance

Francesco Totti

Hometown: Rome, Italy
Club: A.S. Roma

"Totti is the prototype modern player; the first of his kind."

– writer Mario Sconcerti

Observers would think that 2007's Golden Boot winner as Europe's top goalscorer would be awarded to a player at a high-profile program. A striker at Manchester United, or Real Madrid, or Chelsea would be more likely to earn the award than one from internationally minor A.S. Roma. It is there, however, that Europe's leading scorer Francesco Totti plays, and it is there where he will stay.

A close-knit family with strong values and work ethic, the Tottis were naturally gifted at soccer. After youth stints around the country, Francesco would mature into a strong player for A.S. Roma, his hometown team. Living with his family and enjoying his mother's home cooking has proven to be the right recipe for one of the world's under-appreciated stars.

That's not to say that Totti has been ignored by pundits and fans, most notably being named to Pele's select list of the world's greatest living players, the FIFA 100. Fans throughout Italy, however, have long been aware of Totti's finesse and nose for the ball; he is Roma's all-time leading scorer and is the most-capped player in the club's history.

Internationally, Totti was nearly kept out of the 2006 World Cup due to a broken ankle. Playing with plates and screws holding it together, Totti turned in some key perform- ances in front of a world-wide audience. He would score the decisive goal in the waning moments against Australia, provide a key assist against the Ukraine, and play the entirety of Italy's semifinal win over Germany. He would last over an hour into the final with France, and when the tournament ended in penalty kicks, Totti would be both an interna- tionally known name and a World Champion.

Teams that Totti has played for in his career

Ht: 5' 11" • **Wt:** 175 • **DOB:** 9/27/76

Position: Midfield/Striker

2007–2008 Salary: $7.8 million

Career Goals/International caps: 165 goals/58 caps

Personal Homepage: www.francescototti.com

Did you know?: Totti played in the 2006 World Cup despite having screws in his ankle.

As a kid: Francesco comes from a very close family that was very supportive. They all still lived together until recently.

Fun tidbit: Although he never made it as a professional player, Totti says that his brother was the better player growing up.

Hobbies: Francesco owns a soccer school and a motorcycle racing team.

Favorite music: Pop and classical

Cuauhtemoc Blanco

Hometown: Mexico City
Club: Chicago Fire

Intense is too soft of a word to describe Cuauhtemoc Blanco on the soccer field. Any fan who has ever seen him play can never forget the sight: back hunched over, pacing down the field with an artistic flair that is belied by his odd appearance while in motion. Demonstrative and never lacking for words on the pitch, referees and opposing players bear much of the brunt of the Chicago Fire star's anger on the field.

Blanco is truly one of a kind to watch play. A legend in his home country of Mexico and one of the most high-profile stars in MLS, he is reserved off the field but anything but reserved on it. Scorching free kicks combine with amazing touch and creativity, giving the Fire one of the world's most unique soccer players.

A fixture for 15 years at Club America in Mexico, Blanco is now in his second season in MLS, playing as hard as ever. A common fixture in Mexico's lineup for international play as well, Blanco has appeared in two World Cups during his career.

After Mexico's 1–0 win over Canada on September 10, 2008, Blanco announced that he was retiring from international soccer. Although his career is beginning to wind towards its end, Blanco has said that he wishes to spend a few more seasons with the Fire before playing his final season back home in Mexico. Until then, fans in the United States will be treated to seeing one of the most passionate players in the world.

"Every time we travel people support him and the team and it is great for us."
—Fire captain Chris Armas

Fast Stat:

4

Mexican MVP awards Blanco won during his time in the Primera Division

Ht: 5' 10" • **Wt:** 170 • **DOB:** 1/17/73

Position: Midfield

2008–2009 Salary: $2.6 million

Career Goals/International caps:
155 club goals/100 international caps

Personal Homepage:
www.cuauhtemoc-blanco.com

Did you know?: Blanco retired from international soccer on September 10, 2008.

As a kid: Blanco grew up in a rough neighborhood, and played soccer as a way to avoid the violence around him.

Fun tidbit: When he is done playing for the Fire, Blanco wants to return to his old club, America, to finish his career.

Hobbies: Cuauhtemoc is very active in helping out children in need, such as participating in ESPN's "My Wish."

Favorite music: Blanco enjoys traditional Mexican music and pop

David Trezeguet

Hometown: Rouen, France
Club: Juventus

98

Speed, in miles per hour, of a goal Trezeguet scored in the Champions League in 1997. It's the fastest recorded speed of any goal in that competition.

Ht: 6' 3" • **Wt:** 175 • **DOB:** 10/15/77

Position: Striker

2008–2009 Salary: $6.5 million

Career Goals/International caps:
182 club goals/71 international caps

Personal Homepage:
www.trezegol.com

Did you know?: David's father, Jorge, played for the Argentina national team.

As a kid: David was born in France, but grew up in Argentina.

Fun tidbit: One of David's best friends is Thierry Henry of Barcelona. They met while playing together at Monaco.

Hobbies: Along with many Brazilian players, David enjoys playing beach soccer even though he is not Brazilian.

Favorite music: David enjoys samba music and other South American styles.

Considered among soccer connoisseurs to be one of the most underrated players in the world, David Trezeguet may not be a household name in America, but he is one of the top players in the world. Having scored 130 career goals in just over 200 games for Juventus in Italy, Trezeguet's scoring touch is almost unmatched in Europe.

Born to Argentinean player Jorge Trezeguet and his wife while he was playing professionally in France, David Trezeguet aspired from an early age to play professionally in Europe. After starting his career in Argentina, Trezeguet had trials with several French clubs. At first it looked like he might not get a chance to play in Europe, but AS Monaco decided to sign the young Trezeguet (although Monaco is an independent country, the soccer club plays in the French league). Forming a dynamite tandem with fellow Frenchman Thierry Henry, Monaco remained near the top of French soccer. Trezeguet next took his game to Italy, where he is a goal-scoring force for Juventus.

Trezeguet was a big part of the French national team for nearly a decade. He was part of France's victorious 1998 World Cup squad and scored a golden goal to give France a championship at Euro 2000. He also represented France at the World Cup in 2002 and 2006 before retiring from international soccer in 2008.

More recently, Trezeguet has remained a top scorer in Serie A. Last season he put in 20 goals, second in the league only to teammate Alessandro del Piero.

"David is one of the most underrated strikers in the world"
— Thierry Henry

Lukas Podolski

Hometown: Gliwice, Poland
Club: Bayern Munich

Lukas Podolski has had an interesting rise in the soccer world. A Polish-born but distinctly German striker, Podolski made a name for himself thanks to a stirring performance in the 2006 World Cup, oddly enough while his club team sat mired in the second division.

In fact, Podolski was the first German in decades to become a regular on the national team while playing in the second division. Indeed, it is rare to see a talent on any national team that is competitive in the world that plays second division soccer.

Although Podolski had once rescued his Cologne team from the doldrums to the Bundesliga, he would not be around to do it a second time. His performance in Germany's ultimate third-place finish was enough to secure him a transfer, and a big payday, to Bayern Munich, a dominating force in German soccer.

Again, Podolski has shined brightest on an international stage, this time in the Champion's League. Saving some of his best performances for Bayern's key games in the competition, Lukas Podolski is quickly becoming one of the best big-game strikers in the world of soccer. In 2006, Podolski became just the third German to ever score 4 goals in an international game, showcasing even more of the potential that he has yet to tap into.

"Lukas Podolski is a great performer and we have to let him do what he can."

– German keeper Jens Lehmann during the 2006 World Cup

Fast Stat:

2

Podolski is one of two Polish-born players on the German national team.

Ht: 5' 11" • **Wt:** 170 • **DOB:** 6/4/85

Position: Striker

2007–2008 Salary: $11.9 million

Career Goals/International caps:
55 goals/46 caps

Personal Homepage:
www.lukas-podolski.com

Did you know?: Lukas was born in Poland but his family moved to Germany when he was still a toddler.

Fun tidbit: Lukas appeared on the cover of FIFA 07 in Germany.

Hobbies: Basketball and music

Favorite music: Lukas will listen to anything, but enjoys dance.

Landon Donovan

Hometown: Ontario, California
Club: Los Angeles Galaxy

Perhaps the biggest star of United States soccer in this generation, Landon Donovan has had a roller-coaster career. From his pedigree with the national team development program to disaster in Europe, to a rebirth back home, the 26-year-old Donovan has already had enough ups and downs for an entire career.

Unlike most players in the United States, Donovan never played college soccer. Going pro at age 18 instead, he figured heavily in the future plans of German squad Bayer Leverkusen. To further season Donovan, they returned him on loan to the San Jose Earthquakes of the MLS to get game experience.

Donovan would become a star in San Jose, quickly proving himself as a dangerous offensive threat. He would star for the U.S. team at the 2000 Olympics in Australia and would become a full member of the national squad later that year.

Landon would figure heavily in the U.S. run in the 2002 World Cup, finding the back of the net twice. With his career on the rise, Bayer decided to recall him from loan in 2005. The Bundesliga, however, would not be kind to Donovan and he would make just seven appearances for the team before being sold to MLS.

He would quickly find himself allocated to the LA Galaxy, and immediately establish himself as a leader on the squad. Playing with David Beckham and with another World Cup under his belt, Landon led the MLS in scoring in 2008 with 20 goals.

"Anything with the ball is the best thing you can do, everything else will come to you later, just be with the ball as much as possible."

— Landon's advice to young players

Fast Stat:

35

International goals scored by Donovan, the most all-time for the U.S.

Ht: 5' 8" • **Wt:** 175 • **DOB:** 3/4/82

Position: Midfield/Striker

2007–2008 Salary: $900,000

Career Goals/International caps: 87 goals/100 caps

Did you know?: The entire time Donovan played for the San Jose Earthquakes, he was on loan from his German club.

As a kid: Landon played with several U.S. teammates with the national team development program in Bradenton, Florida.

Favorite foods: Crab meat

Hobbies: Landon enjoys outdoor activities and travel.

Favorite music: Landon will listen to anything, especially when it comes to getting pumped up for a game.

David Villa

Hometown: Langrea, Spain

Club: Valencia

The son of a coal miner, David Villa dreamed of a life without heading down into the mines. A star from a young age, he has quickly established himself as one of soccer's premier goal scorers. Annually linked with some of the biggest clubs in Europe, Villa has instead helped Valencia become a regular at the top of the Spanish League's standings and in the Champions League.

David began his career in the second division of Spanish soccer, with his hometown club Sporting de Gijon. After scoring nearly 50 goals over three seasons, it became clear that Villa belonged in the top flight, so he was sold to the newly promoted Real Zaragoza. The move up did not faze David, as he scored 17 goals in his first season at the top and led Zaragoza to a Copa del Rey win over Real Madrid.

After Spain began to come calling for Villa's services, Valencia began to take notice of the young striker and bought him in 2005 for 12 million Euros. He finished second in league scoring in his first season with his new club, scoring 25 times in 35 matches. Villa has also helped Valencia become a regular in the Champions League, though they have yet to make it past the quarterfinals.

David is an even bigger star with the Spanish national team, where he has truly showed his world-class ability. With a wide range of young strikers in action at Euro 2008, it was Villa who was better than all, netting four goals in the competition and leading Spain to the championship. No longer the best kept secret of Spain, clubs all over Europe are now clamoring for Villa.

Fast Stat:

4

Goals David scored at Euro 2008, the most for any player at the tournament

Ht: 5' 9" • **Wt:** 160 • **DOB:** 12/3/1981

Position: Striker

2008–2009 Salary: $2.78 million

Career Goals/International caps: 141 club goals/33 caps

Did you know?: In 2006, David scored three goals in less than five minutes against Athletic Bilbao.

As a kid: David's career almost ended before it even began: when he was nine years old he shattered his leg, but thanks to his doctors, he was able to play soccer again.

Fun tidbit: In 2005, David and his wife Patricia had their first child, a girl named Zaida.

Hobbies: David enjoys sleeping during the season and travelling during the offseason.

Favorite music: David enjoys traditional Spanish music and the Valencia FC songs.

*"David Villa is one of Europe's
most lethal finishers"*

– Spain manager Luis Aragones

"[Toni] was priceless in terms of the way Italy played."

– Italy striker Paolo Rossi after the 2006 World Cup

Luca Toni

Hometown:
Pavullo nel Frignano, Italy

Club: Bayern Munich

Journeyman Luca Toni was a fixture of the lower divisions of Italian soccer for nearly a decade, a player at the top end of the second level seemingly for his entire career. A timely promotion for his club and a solid season in the top flight, however, has turned Toni into one of the premier Italian strikers. One season of his work even remains one of the best seasons of any striker in European history.

The 2005–2006 season was the magic year for Luca Toni, and one of the best of any player in Italian league history. Toni scored early and scored often, piling in 31 goals over the course of the season, easily winning the Serie A Golden Boot. He was the first player to score 30 goals in the league since the 1950s, and because of the formula used to calculate the winner, was named the European Golden Boot winner as well. Fiorentina had a strong season as well, finishing fourth in the league and qualifying for the Champions League (though they were later stripped of this honor for their role in a match-fixing scandal).

After moving to Bayern Munich in a deal worth 11 million Euros, Toni has continued to have success. Although he hasn't reached his 2005–2006 pace since, he remains a feared striker. He has recorded a hat trick for Bayern and scored both of the team's goals in their German Cup win in 2007.

Toni has played for the Italian national team since 2004, a late debut. He scored two goals in the 2006 World Cup, but has fallen off of form lately, struggling at Euro 2008.

Fast Stat:

10

Clubs that Luca Toni has played for in his career

Ht: 6' 4" • **Wt:** 175 • **DOB:** 5/26/77

Position: Striker

2008–2009 Salary: $8 million

Career Goals/International caps:
186 club goals/33 international caps

Personal Homepage: www.lucatoni.com

Did you know?: Last year, Luca Toni scored four goals in one game during the UEFA Cup.

As a kid: A late bloomer, it took Luca several years to grow into his frame after an early growth spurt propelled him to six feet, four inches.

Favorite food: Fish and traditional Italian dishes.

Hobbies: Luca enjoys reading and doing puzzles in his spare time.

Favorite music: American rock music and anything to get him pumped up before a game.

Player Stats

David Villa

Season	Club	Country	Level	GP	GS
2007-08	Valencia	ESP	A	28	18
2006-07	Valencia	ESP	A	36	15
2005-06	Valencia	ESP	A	37	25
2004-05	Zaragoza	ESP	A	35	15
2003-04	Zaragoza	ESP	A	38	17
2002-03	Sporting Gijon	ESP	B	39	20
2001-02	Sporting Gijon	ESP	B	40	18
2000-01	Sporting Gijon B	ESP	C	35	13
2000-01	Sporting Gijon	ESP	B	1	0
Career Totals:				289	141

Cesc Fabregas

Season	Club	Country	Level	GP	GS
2007-08	Arsenal	ENG	A	31	7
2006-07	Arsenal	ENG	A	38	2
2005-06	Arsenal	ENG	A	35	3
2004-05	Arsenal	ENG	A	33	2
2003-04	Arsenal	ENG	A	0	0
2002-03	FC Barcelona B	ESP	C	0	0
Career Totals:				137	14

Cuauhtemoc Blanco

Season	Club	Country	Level	GP	GS
2007-07	Chicago Fire	USA	A	17	4
2006-07	America	MEX	A	36	13
2005-06	America	MEX	A	28	7
2004-05	America	MEX	A	20	8
2004-05	Veracruz	MEX	A	15	5
2003-04	America	MEX	A	38	20
2002-03	America	MEX	A	36	11
2001-02	Valladolid	ESP	A	20	3
2000-01	Valladolid	ESP	A	3	0
1999-00	America	MEX	A	36	20
1998-99	America	MEX	A	31	31
1997-98	Necaxa	MEX	A	28	13
1996-97	America	MEX	A	27	9
1995-96	America	MEX	A	29	5
1994-95	America	MEX	A	28	6
1993-94	America	MEX	A	4	0
1992-93	America	MEX	A	12	0
Career Totals:				408	155

Iker Casillas

Season	Club	Country	Level	GP	GS
2007-08	Real Madrid	ESP	A	36	0
2006-07	Real Madrid	ESP	A	38	0
2005-06	Real Madrid	ESP	A	37	0
2004-05	Real Madrid	ESP	A	37	0
2003-04	Real Madrid	ESP	A	37	0
2002-03	Real Madrid	ESP	A	38	0
2001-02	Real Madrid	ESP	A	25	0
2000-01	Real Madrid	ESP	A	34	0
1999-00	Real Madrid	ESP	A	27	0
1999-00	Real Madrid B	-	-	4	0
1998-99	Real Madrid C	-	-	0	0
Career Totals:				313	0

Player Stats

David Trezeguet

Season	Club	Country	Level	GP	GS
2007-08	Juventus	ITA	A	36	20
2006-07	Juventus	ITA	B	31	15
2005-06	Juventus	ITA	A	32	23
2004-05	Juventus	ITA	A	18	9
2003-04	Juventus	ITA	A	25	16
2002-03	Juventus	ITA	A	17	9
2001-02	Juventus	ITA	A	34	24
2000-01	Juventus	ITA	A	25	14
1999-00	Monaco	FRA	A	30	22
1998-99	Monaco	FRA	A	27	12
1997-98	Monaco	FRA	A	27	18
1996-97	Monaco	FRA	A	5	0
1995-96	Monaco	FRA	A	4	0
1994-95	Platense	-	-	2	0
1993-94	Platense	-	-	3	0
Career Totals:				316	182

Luca Toni

Season	Club	Country	Level	GP	GS
2007-08	Bayern Munchen	GER	A	31	24
2006-07	Fiorentina	ITA	A	29	16
2005-06	Fiorentina	ITA	A	38	31
2004-05	Palermo	ITA	A	35	21
2003-04	Palermo	ITA	B	45	30
2002-03	Brescia	ITA	A	16	2
2001-02	Brescia	ITA	A	28	13
2000-01	Vicenza	ITA	A	31	9
1999-00	Treviso	ITA	B	35	15
1998-99	Lodigiani	ITA	C1	31	15
1997-98	Fiorenzuola	ITA	C1	25	2
1996-97	Empoli	ITA	B	3	1
1995-96	Modena	ITA	C1	25	5
1994-95	Modena	ITA	C1	7	2
Career Totals:				379	186

David Beckham

Season	Club	Country	Level	GP	GS
2007-07	Los Angeles Galaxy	USA	A	5	0
2006-07	Real Madrid	ESP	A	23	3
2005-06	Real Madrid	ESP	A	31	3
2004-05	Real Madrid	ESP	A	30	4
2003-04	Real Madrid	ESP	A	32	3
2002-03	Manchester United	ENG	A	31	6
2001-02	Manchester United	ENG	A	28	11
2000-01	Manchester United	ENG	A	31	9
1999-00	Manchester United	ENG	A	31	6
1998-99	Manchester United	ENG	A	35	6
1997-98	Manchester United	ENG	A	37	9
1996-97	Manchester United	ENG	A	36	7
1995-96	Manchester United	ENG	A	33	7
1994-95	Manchester United	ENG	A	4	0
1994-95	Preston North End	-	-	5	2
1993-94	Manchester United	ENG	A	0	0
1992-93	Manchester United	ENG	A	0	0
Career Totals:				392	76

Player Stats

Kaka

Season	Club	Country	Level	GP	GS
2007-08	Milan	ITA	A	30	15
2006-07	Milan	ITA	A	31	8
2005-06	Milan	ITA	A	35	14
2004-05	Milan	ITA	A	36	7
2003-04	Milan	ITA	A	30	10
2003-03	Sao Paulo	BRA	A	9	2
2002-02	Sao Paulo	BRA	A	22	9
2001-01	Sao Paulo	BRA	A	27	12
Career Totals:				220	77

Ronaldinho

Season	Club	Country	Level	GP	GS
2007-08	FC Barcelona	ESP	A	17	8
2006-07	FC Barcelona	ESP	A	32	21
2005-06	FC Barcelona	ESP	A	29	17
2004-05	FC Barcelona	ESP	A	35	9
2003-04	FC Barcelona	ESP	A	32	15
2002-03	Paris St-Germain	FRA	A	27	8
2001-02	Paris St-Germain	FRA	A	28	9
2000-00	Grîmio	BRA	A	15	8
1999-99	Grîmio	BRA	A	47	22
1998-98	Grîmio	BRA	A	48	7
Career Totals:				310	124

Cristiano Ronaldo

Season	Club	Country	Level	GP	GS
2007-08	Manchester United	ENG	A	34	31
2006-07	Manchester United	ENG	A	34	17
2005-06	Manchester United	ENG	A	33	9
2004-05	Manchester United	ENG	A	33	5
2003-04	Manchester United	ENG	A	29	4
2002-03	Sporting	POR	A	25	3
Career Totals:				188	69

Fernando Torres

Season	Club	Country	Level	GP	GS
2007-08	Liverpool	ENG	A	33	24
2006-07	Atlético Madrid	ESP	A	36	14
2005-06	Atlético Madrid	ESP	A	36	13
2004-05	Atlético Madrid	ESP	A	38	16
2003-04	Atlético Madrid	ESP	A	35	20
2002-03	Atlético Madrid	ESP	A	29	12
2001-02	Atlético Madrid	ESP	B	36	6
2000-01	Atlético Madrid	ESP	B	4	1
Career Totals:				247	106

Lionel Messi

Season	Club	Country	Level	GP	GS
2007-08	FC Barcelona	ESP	A	28	10
2006-07	FC Barcelona	ESP	A	26	14
2005-06	FC Barcelona	ESP	A	17	6
2004-05	FC Barcelona	ESP	A	7	1
2003-04	FC Barcelona B	ESP	C	5	0
Career Totals:				83	31

Landon Donovan

Season	Club	Country	Level	GP	GS
2007-07	Los Angeles Galaxy	USA	A	25	8
2006-06	Los Angeles Galaxy	USA	A	24	12
2005-05	Los Angeles Galaxy	USA	A	26	16
2004-05	Bayer Leverkusen	GER	A	7	0
2004-04	San Jose Earthquakes	USA	A	25	6
2003-03	San Jose Earthquakes	USA	A	26	16
2002-02	San Jose Earthquakes	USA	A	22	8
2001-01	San Jose Earthquakes	USA	A	28	12
2000-01	Bayer Leverkusen II	GER	C	8	3
1999-00	Bayer Leverkusen II	GER	C	20	6
Career Totals:				211	87

Player Stats

Thierry Henry

Season	Club	Games	Goals	Yellow Cards	Red Cards
2007-08	FC Barcelona	ESP	A	30	12
2006-07	Arsenal	ENG	A	17	10
2005-06	Arsenal	ENG	A	32	27
2004-05	Arsenal	ENG	A	32	25
2003-04	Arsenal	ENG	A	37	30
2002-03	Arsenal	ENG	A	37	24
2001-02	Arsenal	ENG	A	33	24
2000-01	Arsenal	ENG	A	35	17
1999-00	Arsenal	ENG	A	31	18
1998-99	Juventus	ITA	A	16	3
1998-99	Monaco	FRA	A	13	1
1997-98	Monaco	FRA	A	30	4
1996-97	Monaco	FRA	A	36	9
1995-96	Monaco	FRA	A	18	3
1994-95	Monaco	FRA	A	8	3
Career Totals:				405	210

Steven Gerrard

Season	Club	Country	Level	GP	GS
2007-08	Liverpool	ENG	A	34	11
2006-07	Liverpool	ENG	A	36	7
2005-06	Liverpool	ENG	A	32	10
2004-05	Liverpool	ENG	A	30	7
2003-04	Liverpool	ENG	A	34	4
2002-03	Liverpool	ENG	A	34	5
2001-02	Liverpool	ENG	A	28	3
2000-01	Liverpool	ENG	A	33	7
1999-00	Liverpool	ENG	A	28	1
1998-99	Liverpool	ENG	A	11	0
Career Totals:				300	55

Michael Ballack

Season	Club	Country	Level	GP	GS
2007-08	Chelsea	ENG	A	18	7
2006-07	Chelsea	ENG	A	26	4
2005-06	Bayern Munchen	GER	A	26	13
2004-05	Bayern Munchen	GER	A	27	13
2003-04	Bayern Munchen	GER	A	28	7
2002-03	Bayern Munchen	GER	A	26	10
2001-02	Bayer Leverkusen	GER	A	29	17
2000-01	Bayer Leverkusen	GER	A	27	7
1999-00	Bayer Leverkusen	GER	A	23	3
1998-99	Kaiserslautern	GER	A	30	4
1997-98	Kaiserslautern	GER	A	16	0
1997-98	Kaiserslautern A	GER	-	17	8
1996-97	Chemnitzer	GER	-	34	10
1995-96	Chemnitzer	GER	-	15	0
Career Totals:				342	103

Wayne Rooney

Season	Club	Country	Level	GP	GS
2007-08	Manchester United	ENG	A	27	12
2006-07	Manchester United	ENG	A	35	14
2005-06	Manchester United	ENG	A	36	16
2004-05	Manchester United	ENG	A	29	11
2003-04	Everton	ENG	A	34	9
2002-03	Everton	ENG	A	33	6
2001-02	Everton	ENG	A	0	0
Career Totals:				194	68

Player Stats

Frank Lampard

Season	Club	Country	Level	GP	GS
2007-08	Chelsea	ENG	A	24	10
2006-07	Chelsea	ENG	A	37	11
2005-06	Chelsea	ENG	A	35	16
2004-05	Chelsea	ENG	A	38	13
2003-04	Chelsea	ENG	A	38	10
2002-03	Chelsea	ENG	A	38	6
2001-02	Chelsea	ENG	A	37	5
2000-01	West Ham	ENG	A	30	7
1999-00	West Ham	ENG	A	34	7
1998-99	West Ham	ENG	A	38	5
1997-98	West Ham	ENG	A	31	4
1996-97	West Ham	ENG	A	13	0
1995-96	West Ham	ENG	A	2	0
1995-96	Swansea City	ENG	C	9	1
Career Totals:				404	95

Francesco Totti

Season	Club	Country	Level	GP	GS
2007-08	Roma	ITA	A	25	14
2006-07	Roma	ITA	A	35	26
2005-06	Roma	ITA	A	23	15
2004-05	Roma	ITA	A	29	12
2003-04	Roma	ITA	A	31	20
2002-03	Roma	ITA	A	24	14
2001-02	Roma	ITA	A	24	8
2000-01	Roma	ITA	A	30	13
1999-00	Roma	ITA	A	27	7
1998-99	Roma	ITA	A	31	12
1997-98	Roma	ITA	A	30	13
1996-97	Roma	ITA	A	26	5
1995-96	Roma	ITA	A	28	2
1994-95	Roma	ITA	A	21	4
1993-94	Roma	ITA	A	8	0
1992-93	Roma	ITA	A	2	0
Career Totals:				394	165

Lukas Podolski

Season	Club	Country	Level	GP	GS
2007-08	Bayern Munchen	GER	A	25	5
2007-08	Bayern Munchen II	GER	C	2	0
2006-07	Bayern Munchen	GER	A	22	4
2005-06	Koln	GER	A	32	12
2004-05	Koln	GER	B	30	24
2003-04	Koln	GER	A	19	10
2003-04	Koln A	GER	C	1	0
2002-03	Koln A	GER	C	1	0
Career Totals:				132	55

Joe Cole

Season	Club	Country	Level	GP	GS
2007-08	Chelsea	ENG	A	33	7
2006-07	Chelsea	ENG	A	13	0
2005-06	Chelsea	ENG	A	34	8
2004-05	Chelsea	ENG	A	28	8
2003-04	Chelsea	ENG	A	35	1
2002-03	West Ham	ENG	A	35	4
2001-02	West Ham	ENG	A	30	0
2000-01	West Ham	ENG	A	30	5
1999-00	West Ham	ENG	A	22	1
1998-99	West Ham	ENG	A	8	0
Career Totals:				268	34